Scream Team

The Vampire at Half Court

by Bill Doyle
Illustrated by Jared Lee

Scholastic Inc.
New York Toronto London Auckland
Sydney Mexico City New Delhi Hong Kong

For T. Michael Doyle, king of the court.
—B.D.

To cousin Ted Fiock.
—J.L.

ISBN 978-0-545-34199-8

12 11 10 9 8 7 6 5 4 3 2   12 13 14 15 16 17/0

Printed in the U.S.A.   40
First printing, March 2012

Book design by Jennifer Rinaldi Windau

CHAPTER 1
Ghoul for It

Karl raced down the court on three paws like a blur of fur. His fourth paw could barely dribble the basketball fast enough to keep up. But he didn't have much farther to go. The path to the net was clear for an easy lay-up.

"Karl, watch out!" Patsy the zombie shouted from behind him. "A ghost is right on your tail!"

Karl waved to his teammate over his shoulder and picked up speed. This was one werewolf who didn't want to get caught—not tonight!

The Scream Team was playing the Ghosts in the second-to-last game of the regular season. So far the Scream Team had won 8 out of 11 games. If they could win tonight and next week, they would play the undefeated Vampires in the JC Monster League Championship. But if the Scream Team lost either of the next two games . . . they'd be out of the running.

"No, really, Karl!" Patsy yelled. "A Ghost is *on* your tail!"

Still dribbling, Karl turned his head and saw it was true. A player from the other team had hitched a ride. Finn the Ghost sat on the tip of Karl's tail and grinned at him.

"Hi, Karl," Finn said, scrunching up his nose. "You should do something about your patchy fur. It's super scratchy."

A flock of whooping-brain monsters in the front row hooted and laughed.

"Get *off*!" Karl flicked his tail but the Ghost held on with both hands.

Karl felt enough pressure as the Scream Team's point guard. He didn't need to be reminded that his fur made him look like a patchy poodle.

Karl snapped his tail again. This time Finn was thrown loose. As the Ghost whooshed by, he snatched the ball from Karl's hands. Finn cackled and zipped the other way down the court, right past the Cyclops referee.

The ref blew his whistle and called, "Traveling!"

"Boo!" shrieked a few of the Ghosts on the bench. But Karl didn't know if he should take the booing personally. They *were* ghosts, after all.

"What are they mad about?" Karl asked his best friend, J.D., who was also a ghost. He played small forward on the Scream Team.

"Same old story." J.D. shrugged. "Ghosts don't

have legs, so how can you tell if one's traveling?"

The Ghosts were still angry when Karl inbounded the ball. Two of them blipped into air for a second and flew right through him. The ref blew the whistle again, calling a personal foul.

From up in the announcer's booth, Hairy Hairwell's voice thundered over the speakers. "Taking two free throws for the Scream Team is Karl the werewolf, number zero!"

"Zero?" a squid creature shouted from the upper bleachers. "Is that Karl's number or the amount of friends he has?"

More laughter came from the crowd as Karl went to the line.

"I can sew a new number on your shirt," said Maxwell the mummy. He was lined up next to Bolt the Frankenstein's monster along the key. Maxwell faced away from the net. As always, the mummy's sweaty, oversized wrapping blocked his eyes.

To make their basketball uniforms, Maxwell had torn the legs off their baseball uniforms from the knee down. Now they had raggedy shorts made of old coffin lining.

"Thanks, Maxwell," Karl said. "I like zero just fine." All the jokes about him and his fur were distracting, but he loved playing too much to let them ruin it. Also, Karl knew the Scream Team was pretty good. Sure, they'd won three games by forfeit when the other teams didn't show up. Only the two squads with the best season records would play in the championship. And his team was so close to being one of them! Other monsters just didn't like that the Scream Team players weren't all the same.

Karl dribbled the ball three and a half times, like he always did before a free throw, took the shot,

and sank it. *Yes!* The score was now 60 to 62. The Scream Team trailed by two points with ninety seconds left to play.

As the ref tossed the ball back to him, Karl thought he saw another Ghost floating behind him.

Sneaky spirit!

Karl growled and started to chase the Ghost away when Patsy threw her arms up to stop him. Her limbs snapped off her shoulders, spun through the air, and plopped down on the floor.

"Easy, Karl," she said, using her feet to screw her arms back on. "That's not a Ghost. It's your tail."

Karl blushed. "Oh, right," he said. Chasing his tail was something he did when he got nervous. Karl tried to focus. But his second shot clanged off the rim and bounced toward half court.

The players scrambled for the ball, bobbling it back and forth until finally Karl grabbed the ball under the Ghosts' net. Both teams ran to the other end of the court, waiting for Karl to bring the ball up.

But Karl had other ideas. *I can win the game right now.*

Instead of heading toward his basket, he dribbled into the tiny space between the back of the Ghosts' backboard and the out-of-bounds line.

"No, Karl!" J.D. yelled, his body turning bright red with alarm. He saw what Karl was up to.

"I don't believe it," Hairy announced. "The Scream Team point guard is going for a Monster Six-Pointer!"

The crowd gasped. To get six points, a player had to shoot the ball from behind one backboard all the way down the court into the other net. It was nearly impossible. Only Karl's hero, the werewolf Wolfenstein, had ever made this full-court shot.

But Karl wanted the Scream Team to win more than anything. They'd be one step closer to playing in the championship game.

"Go for it, Karl!" One voice rose above the others. Actually, the words sounded more like "Sho so fit, Karsh!" because of the drool dripping down the speaker's gigantic fangs. It was the plump vampire Dennis, sitting in his usual spot on the Scream Team bench.

Dennis is right, Karl thought. *I'll go for it! Then maybe everyone will FINALLY stop laughing at us.*

The Ghosts rushed toward Karl like a crashing wave.

Karl concentrated. He released the ball and sent it sailing over the charging Ghosts. All eyes in the stadium followed the ball as it arced toward the other basket.

Crossing his paws, Karl said, "Please, please, please, go in!"

CHAPTER 2
Nothing but Air

Whiff!

The ball came down about three feet from the net. Not even close. Annie the Ghost swept in and dribbled down the court for two points.

"Nice air ball, hair ball!" Annie taunted Karl as laughter rang throughout the stadium.

Wolfsbane! Karl thought. This wasn't the way to win the game. And his two coaches agreed.

"No more showboating, Karl!" Coach Wyatt called from the sidelines.

Coach Virgil chirped, "Just stick to the basics, dude, and you'll be peachy!"

"Peachy?" Wyatt scoffed. "Are we talking about basketball or flavors of lice cream?"

The Scream Team coaches were a two-headed monster who shared one body. The Conundrum brothers argued about everything—from the best earwax sauce to how to coach the team. They didn't even agree on the fact that they were related!

Bringing the ball down the court, Karl glanced at the scoreboard. With thirty seconds left, the Ghosts were up by four points.

Karl faked a throw to Bolt—who stood daydreaming, as always—and hit Patsy with an around-the-back, no-look pass. She took a long three-pointer. As she followed through, her hand broke off and whizzed into the Ghosts' cheering section. The ball went in the net, but her hand bounced on a big bass drum and fired back onto the court, slapping Bolt in the face.

"Hey!" Bolt said, snapping out of his daze. He

picked up Patsy's hand and tossed it back to her just as the Ghosts were inbounding the ball. Without meaning to, he knocked the ball loose from Annie the Ghost. J.D. snagged it and went in for a lay-up.

Just in time! The buzzer sounded, ending the game. The rest of the Scream Team—Dennis, Mike, Eric, and Beck—flew, slithered, rolled, and flippered off the bench and onto the court to celebrate.

Coach Grant of the Ghosts was furious. After rushing through the handshake line, he rocketed over to the Coaches Conundrum with the basketball in his hands.

"This ball you provided for the game has gum in it!" The Ghost coach held out the ball so everyone could see two fang marks plugged up with gum.

Coach Virgil smiled. "Chill, dude. It's still totally bouncy."

"Besides, we had to cover the holes," Coach Wyatt snapped. "Karl here bit it."

Karl blushed again. He had a weakness for chasing squeaky things. But he was getting better at fighting the urge.

"What is all this ruckus?" a voice demanded. The crowd around them parted. Dr. Neuron, head of the JCML, strode onto the court. As usual, his sour face looked like he'd just eaten mush bugs dipped in slime pudding.

"Why is the Scream Team still dressed like this?" He pointed a tentacle at Dennis's torn uniform.

"Ish . . . ush . . ." Dennis mumbled as Dr. Neuron glared at him. Dennis panicked. Tiny bat wings popped out of his back and flapped like a hummingbird's. Still getting the hang of flying, he shot up out of control toward the scoreboard.

With Dennis gone, Dr. Neuron turned his attention to the Coaches Conundrum. "What did I tell you two about your team wearing coffin lining? The JCML has certain standards."

Coach Grant yelled, "This is what happens when you let different kinds of monsters play on the same team!"

Dr. Neuron held up a tentacle for silence. He

thought for a second, squinting at the Scream Team. "Hmmm . . ." he muttered under his breath. "If only there was a way to solve the problems with the Scream Team once and for all. Let me think. . . ."

Dr. Neuron took a pen and the thick league rule book from his pocket. He flipped the book open and scribbled on a random page.

"Why! What's this?" Dr. Neuron said as if he had just discovered something new in the book. "Attention, please!" he said, and waited for the remaining crowd in the stadium to quiet down. Then he read out loud, "'Forthwith hitherto all teams that wish to play in the Junior Club Monster League shall require a sponsor. If such sponsor cannot be found, said team will be forced to leave the JCML forever and ever.'"

"You just wrote that!" Wyatt said.

"I'm afraid you can't prove that," Dr. Neuron said. "And once a rule is in the rule book, it must be followed by all teams."

"No problem," Mike the swamp thing said,

pointing between his toes. "I already have one of those anyway."

"Not *pond sore*." Patsy rolled her eyes. "Dr. Neuron said *sponsor*."

"Silence!" Dr. Neuron shouted, finally losing his cool. He put his tentacles over his mouth as if trying to keep from screaming at the Scream Team.

He stormed off with Coach Grant. The Coaches Conundrum followed close behind, trying to get Dr. Neuron to change his mind.

Alone on the court, the Scream Team gathered around Karl. "What's the big deal about getting a sponsor?" Mike asked.

"A sponsor helps pay for a team's equipment," Patsy explained. "Then the team wears the sponsor's name on their uniforms. Like company names on dragsters in Monster Cars."

J.D. shook his head. "That's the problem. Who is going to want to pay so that we can play?"

"We've got to find someone," Karl answered. "Or . . ."

"Or what?" Mike asked.

Just then Dennis fell to the ground with a *splat*.

"That's right, Dennis," Karl said. "We'll fall flat on our faces. It will be the end of the Scream Team."

CHAPTER 3
Overpassed and Passed Over

Two nights later, Karl and the rest of the Scream Team headed to the stadium for practice just like they always did. But this time the building was locked up tight.

They pounded on the door. Finally, a security guard stuck his head out and barked, "By order of Dr. Neuron, no team may enter the stadium without a sponsor." Then he sprayed them with a snot hose until they ran off.

"You know what would be totally cosmic?"

Virgil asked once they'd ducked around the corner and wiped off the boogers. "We could hold practice back at our mansion!"

"Never!" Wyatt shook his head. "That'd be a perfect chance for a spy to sneak into our house."

With no place else to go, the Coaches Conundrum led the team to a mucky spot under Tripleterror Bridge. Mike the swamp thing loved rolling around in the steamy piles of slippery mold. But when Karl tried dribbling the ball, it stuck to the soft ground with a *thwaaack!*

"Don't worry, Scream Team," Coach Virgil said. "We've practiced in worse spots before."

"Oh, I'd worry," Coach Wyatt contradicted. "Even the trolls have moved out from under this bridge."

While the team waded through the goop practicing their sprints, the Conundrums worked on making a poster to get a sponsor. After a few minutes, they held up their sign.

"It's totally spectacular, right?" Virgil asked.

Karl thought the main message—WILL U B R SPONSOR?—was okay. But it had little notes scribbled all around it:

Virgil is a poster poser!

I have a ConunDUMB twin!

Wanted: New Brother

Lost: Marbles . . . please return to my twin

The Conundrums told the team to keep practicing and took the poster to the top of the bridge. Karl peeked up over the side to see them yelling at each other and waving the sign like crazy. The monsters driving by didn't even slow down.

Ducking back below the bridge, Karl asked, "Why isn't anyone stopping?"

"Would *you* stop for us, Karl?" Patsy said. She pointed at Beck the bigfoot, whose flipper-sized feet had clogged the sewage drain, making the slime rise even higher. Maxwell's wrapping blocked his eyes so he didn't know he was bossing around a muck castle built by Bolt. And Dennis was eating handfuls of fat goop flies when no one was looking.

"Stop for us?" Karl shook his head. "I think I'd speed up."

"If we don't get a sponsor, we can't play basketball," said J.D., drifting over to them. "And that means no Scream Team and no championship game . . ."

". . . which means we'll go back to being losers," Patsy finished.

Not going to happen, Karl thought. And an idea hit him. "Why are we waiting for sponsors to come to us?" he said. "We should go to them! We can go to the stores on Mange Street and find a sponsor. The coaches won't even notice we're gone."

The other monsters all agreed. Karl grabbed the ball and they headed to Mange Street. It was lined with giant pus-bag trees, rows of shops, and—

Karl stopped in his tracks. The other teams who needed sponsors had the same idea as the Scream Team. Packs of monsters crisscrossed Mange Street. The Zombies rushed into the video game shop and the Frankenstein's Monsters lumbered into the hardware store.

There was only one store that still looked empty. "Turducken's Butcher Shop!" Karl shouted. "Come on!"

Inside, a horse-bodied monster, Mrs. Turducken, wore a white work bib. "*Hay* there," she snickered from behind the meat counter. "What can I do for you?"

"It's more what we can do for you!" Maxwell said like a monster in a TV ad. "Are you ready for the deal of a lifetime? We will let you put your name on our uniforms and be our sponsor!"

Mrs. Turducken didn't seem interested. Before she could kick them out, Karl said to his friends, "Let's show Mrs. Turducken how the Scream Team works." He pointed to an open meat freezer at the end of the store. "That will be the basket."

He thought they could run through some passing and shooting drills. Mrs. Turducken would see how good they were.

"Karl!" Dennis shouted, spit flying. "I'm open!"

Karl shook his head. He never passed to Dennis. He was Karl's friend. But he always dropped the ball or messed up. And they *really* needed a sponsor.

So Karl passed to Mike, who tried showing off by catching the ball with his slimy tail. The ball slipped off and flew into the air.

"I got it!" Dennis yelled. He grabbed the ball and started toward the freezer as if he was going to slam-dunk it. "Trust me, Karl, I can do this!"

"No, wait, Dennis!" Karl yelled.

Dennis hesitated. Just then the bell over the door rang and the Bigfoot team stuffed themselves into the store. They were clearly looking for a sponsor, too, and elbowed one another with sneaky grins.

Dennis started dribbling again when the biggest Bigfoot smirked. "Hi, Mrs. Turducken! How about a nice, juicy . . . *steak*!"

"Yeah," another Bigfoot chimed in, "do you have any great big *steaks*?"

"Did they say *stake*?" Dennis had stopped dribbling and was looking around wide-eyed. "There are stakes? Here?"

"That's right!" Mrs. Turducken said. "I've got huge steaks! Would you like to have one?"

Dennis's eyes bulged.

"Just laugh it off, Dennis!" Patsy told him. "Laugh and ignore them!"

But Dennis was too freaked out, and scampered out the door, taking the ball with him. When Karl and the rest of the Scream Team got outside, Dennis was still shaking.

"Stakes!" Dennis blubbered. "Sorry I ran out, but why would they talk about stakes to a vampire?"

Karl explained what kind of *steaks* they meant. Once Dennis was calm, Karl reached for the door to the butcher shop. "Let's try that again," he said.

"Too late," Beck groaned. Through the window they could see the Bigfoot team talking happily with Mrs. Turducken. As if to see what it would look like when sewn on, she was spelling the shop's name in raw bologna on their backs.

"She's going to sponsor them instead of us," Maxwell said. "Now what?"

"There!" Karl pointed down the street. "Mr. Medusa's House of Statues!"

"You guys go ahead," Dennis said, giving the ball to Karl. "I need to catch my breath."

Karl and the others got to Mr. Medusa's store just as the Blob team rolled up and pushed in front of them. The store was too crowded—so the Scream Team had to wait outside and peer through the window.

Inside, the Blobs bounced a basketball off one another like they were high-speed bumpers in a pinball machine. The snakes on Mr. Medusa's head cheered as the ball ricocheted here and there at blinding speed. Within seconds, Karl knew the Scream Team had lost out on this sponsor, too. They just couldn't compete.

"Maybe having the same monsters on a team isn't so bad," Patsy said, turning away from the window. "Did you see how the Blobs worked together? We never do that!"

Eric quivered in agreement, and Maxwell asked, "Now what do we do? We don't have a sponsor yet."

Karl was too distracted to answer. At the end of a nearby alley, Dennis was talking to a group of monsters who lurked in the shadows. Karl squinted and could see it was the Vampires, with their slicked-back hair and shiny black uniforms. What were they doing on Mange Street? Like a few other top teams, they already had a sponsor.

Karl strained his wolf ears to hear what Dennis and the Vampires were talking about. He couldn't quite hear them.

Beck spotted Dennis, too. "Hey, Dennis!" he shouted. "What's up?"

The shout startled the Vampires. With a *poof* they turned into bats and disappeared in a flapping cloud down the alley.

"Who you talking to, Dennis?" Mike called.

"No one," Dennis said, looking away. "Uh, I wasn't talking to anyone."

The others nodded. But not Karl. He frowned.

Why is Dennis lying?

CHAPTER 4
V.I.P. from F.I.B.

Karl and the rest of the Scream Team got a text from Dennis the next night:

Meeth me ath the stadium. I have a shurprise.

Even texting, Dennis's words were drooly.

When the team and the Conundrums got to the stadium, they waited outside. The door opened—and the Scream Team ducked. But instead of a guard with a snot hose, it was Dennis! And he was grinning. "What are you doing out here?"

"What are you doing *in* there?" Coach Wyatt asked.

"Come see." He stepped back. They quickly filed inside the dark gym. "Ta-da!" Dennis said, and hit the lights. A mole man wearing a backpack stood at the far end of the court, surrounded by five wooden crates. His long, droopy whiskers curved down his face and onto his shoulders.

"This is Mr. Benedict," Dennis announced. "And guess what? He wants to be our sponsor!"

The Scream Team cheered. Karl pumped his fist in the air and Eric did a happy bounce. Coach Wyatt was the only one who wasn't excited.

"He looks like a spy to me," he said. But Virgil shook Mr. Benedict's hand with a grin. "This is monstrous! How did you find him, Dennis?"

"Um," Dennis said, "he kind of found—"

"I have a store called Fantastic Innovative Basketball?" Mr. Benedict interrupted in a low, raspy voice. "You might know my store better as F.I.B.?" For some reason, Mr. Benedict made every sentence sound like a question.

"I've never heard of it. Where is it?" Karl asked.

"My store is located at . . ." Mr. Benedict mumbled and trailed off. His whiskers twitched. He pulled them tight and plucked them like a mini guitar. *Ping! Ping! Ping!*

"Sorry, Mr. Benedict," Karl said. "I didn't hear where your store is."

"That's too bad," Mr. Benedict said, "because I bet you'd love it . . . if you could find it."

"I bet I would!" Virgil chirped.

"You sap," Wyatt said. "He's a spy!"

"Oh brother." Virgil laughed. "Here we go again. You thought the soda you drank at lunch was a spy."

Wyatt's face went red. "That soda got me to talk!"

"It made you burp!" Virgil laughed harder.

Dennis looked nervous. "Why does it matter how Mr. Benedict got here? He's a sponsor and now we can keep playing basketball!"

"Dennis is right," J.D. said. "We play the Tuna Monsters this weekend. They haven't won a game all season. We'll win with no problem and we'll be in the championship."

Karl couldn't shake the feeling that something wasn't right. But he knew Dennis was trying to be a bigger part of the team. So he let it drop. Meanwhile, the coaches were arguing over Mr. Benedict.

"A mole man?" Wyatt said to his twin. "You do know moles are notorious spies, don't you?"

"Don't look now, dude," Virgil said, "but you've got a mole on your cheek!"

With Wyatt swatting at the freckle on his face, the Conundrums wandered to the corner and kept fighting. Before the team could follow, Mr. Benedict said, "I have presents for you, Scream Team."

Karl and the others turned around. Eric quivered with excitement and made a little squeaky sound. Mr. Benedict opened the lid of one of the crates behind him and reached inside. "I brought these from F.I.B. for you!"

He handed out new high-tops to everyone. They were bright orange and had large platform heels . . . with taps on them.

"Don't tap dancers wear these?" Mike asked.

"Yes, of course." Mr. Benedict nodded. "They will allow you to . . ." He thought for a second, then added, ". . . tap into more basketball energy. As your sponsor, I'll have uniforms for you with all the bells and whistles. But right now, it's snack time!"

From his backpack, he pulled out vinegar-and-broccoli-butter sandwiches on green-fuzz bread.

"From this point on, these sandwiches are all the Scream Team will eat."

Mr. Benedict insisted that each monster finish at least two sandwiches. They formed a ball in Karl's stomach and he could see clumps of them rolling around in J.D.'s belly.

"Isn't this the best?" Dennis sputtered, sinking his huge fangs into his fifth sandwich. Karl had seen Dennis chew on driftwood, so he knew he wasn't a picky eater.

When Karl asked Mr. Benedict if he wanted a sandwich, the mole man shivered.

"Oh no!" Mr. Benedict moaned as if the idea made him want to throw up. And then he quickly made his voice cheerier. "I always eat dinner at the Road Kill Café. Let's practice."

Mr. Benedict tossed out a new basketball.

"You're right-pawed," he said to Karl, "so you need a right-handed basketball."

"There's a difference?" Patsy asked.

"Oh, sure!" Mr. Benedict said.

Karl didn't think that made sense. He kept hoping the Conundrums would come back and take over again. But they were still arguing over in the corner, going in circles. One brother would take a step back toward the team and the other would step away. They went around and around. And everyone else was too riled up about having a sponsor and getting presents—and a little sick from the food— to ask any more questions.

Karl had a bad feeling about this . . . and it wasn't just from the sandwiches gurgling in his stomach.

CHAPTER 5
Saved by the Net

"I'm not going out there dressed like this, Karl," Patsy said. The Scream Team was on the ramp under the stands that led to the court. Their game against the Tunas was about to start.

"What is the problem, Patsy?" Maxwell asked. "I think the uniforms are flattering."

"Seriously?" Patsy shifted Maxwell's wrapping so he could see his reflection in a glass door.

"Ahh!" Maxwell shrieked. "I can look good in anything—except maybe this."

Mr. Benedict hadn't been kidding about the uniforms. They actually had bells and whistles. Bells dangled like fringe from the shorts and mini whistles ran all along the arms. The smallest movement sent the bells clanging and whistles whistling.

"I feel like a one-monster band," Mike said. The whole team was teetering on the platform tap shoes and wearing long capes.

"Where are Coach Wyatt and Coach Virgil?" Karl said, looking around. "They can ask Mr. Benedict to give back our old uniforms."

"I just got a text from the coaches," J.D. said, holding up his cell phone. "But I have no idea what it means."

Karl read the screen, which said:

MVRIBRWGIILLLLIBSEATSHUEPCROEAM-CEHNTIONDNAYY

"Oh yes," Maxwell said. "I believe that's the ancient language of the Balderdash Babblers."

"Uh, I don't think so," Patsy said. "Looks like the coaches are using their two hands to text at the same time. You have to take every other letter to read the two messages."

The first message said, *Mr. B. will be the coach today.* And the second read, *Virgil is a supreme ninny.*

"Wolfsbane," Karl muttered. "The coaches must be fighting harder than ever. They've never missed a game before. . . ."

Just then Mr. Benedict lumbered up the ramp toward them.

"Hey, Mr. Benedict," Dennis said. "Looks like you're our coach tonight!"

"Oh, really?" the mole man said, but didn't sound surprised. "Well, we only have two minutes before the game starts. Better warm up!"

He shooed the team onto the court. But Bolt suddenly stopped next to the team's bench. "No play," he grunted.

"What?" Karl demanded. "What do you mean?"

Bolt looked upset. "No play," he repeated and shook his head.

When Bolt wouldn't say more, Beck explained,

"Mr. Benedict told Bolt to get in touch with the basketball's feelings. 'What's the basketball thinking?' You know, stuff like that."

The rest of the Scream Team shook their heads. No, they didn't know.

"No push ball's face in floor," Bolt said. "Too mean."

"I guess I can understand." Mike nodded. "I wouldn't want someone to dribble my head on the floor either."

"It's no big deal," Patsy said. She popped off her head and tried to dribble it. It wasn't bouncy, so she bounced Eric the blob instead. He splatted on the ground like a cup of gelatin. Bolt wasn't convinced.

"Mr. Benedict," Karl said, "can you tell Bolt that basketballs can't feel anything?"

"Oh?" Mr. Benedict said. "I wouldn't be so sure, you know, because . . ." His voice dropped into a mumble. Then he plucked his whiskers.

Bolt took a seat on the bench and refused to budge. The team needed a different center.

Dennis waved his hand. "I'll go in for Bolt!"

"Um, no," Mr. Benedict said. "That's not the deal. Beck will take Bolt's place."

Dennis didn't argue. He just nodded.

Deal? Karl wondered. *What's that all about?*

Karl was about to head out to the court as point guard when Mr. Benedict shook his head. "Take a seat, Karl," he said. "We're going with a different starting team tonight."

Beck, Eric, and Mike tottered out to the court with Patsy and Maxwell—on their high-top shoes. *Tap! Tap! Tap!*

When the referee tossed up the ball to start the game, Beck jumped for it. He tried to flap his big feet for more air. That just made the tapping louder, like a jackhammer.

Brian the Tuna soared up and flicked the ball with his back fin. But Mike's tail intercepted it before the Tuna's teammates could grab the ball.

Maybe we can do this! Karl thought. *Maybe we can win!*

"Time-out!" Mr. Benedict shouted. One second had clicked off on the clock. The Scream Team rushed back over to the bench. Mr. Benedict stared at them. "Um . . . ?"

"Yes?" Karl prompted. "What is it?"

"Huh, I can't remember why I called time-out," the mole man said. With the time-out over, the Scream Team went back out to the court. Beck was about to inbound the ball.

"Time-out!" Mr. Benedict shouted. Again. But when they huddled around him he still couldn't remember why.

"Is he serious with this?" Patsy muttered to Karl.

When Mr. Benedict called the third time-out, he said, "Now I know what I wanted to say. . . ." They all waited.

"Go ahead," Karl said.

"Go out there and play a good game!" Mr. Benedict finally said.

"We would if you'd let us!" Patsy yelled, her eyes bugging so far out that they popped out of her head.

"Now we don't have any more time-outs!"

"You don't need time-outs," Mr. Benedict said. "You need energy!" And he stuck a broccoli-butter-and-vinegar sandwich in Patsy's mouth.

Back on the court, Beck raised his paw to make the signal for a pick and roll play.

"No!" Mr. Benedict called. "You have to say the play out loud!"

"But then the Tunas will know what we're doing!" Beck called back.

"Not if you call all our plays backward, like we practiced!" Mr. Benedict instructed. "It's the new Scream Team way!"

Beck seemed to realize he didn't have a choice. J.D. thought for a second about what *pick and roll* would be backward and called from the bench, "Llor dna kcip!"

"Is that a riddle?" Mike asked, not realizing Maxwell was passing him the ball. "I don't understand." *Bonk!* The ball hit Mike in the head.

Any other team in the JCML would have

destroyed the Scream Team that night. The monsters couldn't move in their heavy capes and tap shoes. And they had to keep stopping to figure out how to say plays backward.

Luckily, the Tunas had their own problems. Each time they flopped close to the net, they would scream and flop in the other direction. Then they would huddle in a slimy heap in the center of the court.

"What's wrong with them?" Karl asked J.D.

"They're freaked out by nets," J.D. explained. "They *are* tuna monsters."

The game turned into a nightmare—and not the good kind. The Scream Team stumbled around while the Tunas were too scared to get near the basket.

Now Karl knew why the Tunas had the worst record in the JCML.

No one had made a single basket, making the score 0 to 0 at halftime. During the break, the ref warned the Tunas that they couldn't just flop around all game. They were about to set the league record

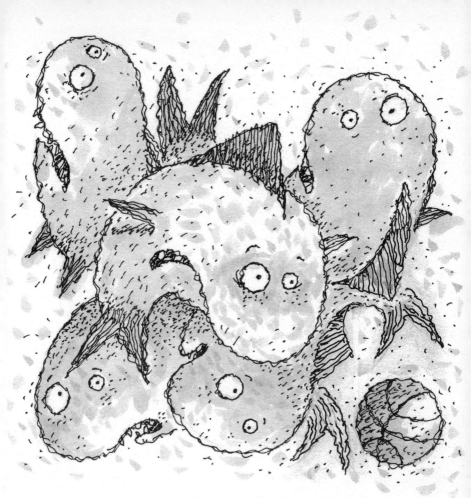

for back-court violations. Rather than risk getting near the nets, the Tunas refused to leave the locker room for the second half.

"The Scream Team wins by forfeit," the ref announced. "They will play the Vampires in the championship game this weekend."

"Victory is ours!" Dennis yelled. "See? I told you Mr. Benedict knew what he was doing!"

Mr. Benedict looked shocked. "You mean the Scream Team won?" he asked, and then answered his own question just as quickly. "Well, of course the Scream Team won. It was all part of my plan!"

All part of his plan? Karl thought as he tapped his way to the locker room. He knew it wasn't just Dennis who was lying anymore. Mr. Benedict was on the list, too.

CHAPTER 6
Undercover Werewolf

Four nights later, Patsy, J.D., Maxwell, and Bolt were up in Karl's tree fort in his backyard.

That was where Karl did his best thinking. There was a poster of his hero, Wolfenstein, on the wall. Each sports season, he changed it. This one showed Wolfenstein sailing over Earwacks to throw down an in-your-face dunk.

He also kept his sports collection up there. He had sealed jars of amazing stuff, like the behind-the-knee sweat from Bonelessness and an actual

rotten molar from Fungitooth.

"Yum," Bolt said, reaching for one of the jars. "Snacks!"

"Don't!" Karl said. Too late. Bolt unscrewed the lid of the jar with five-year-old nacho cheese dip from Putridge Stadium in it.

The stench filled the tree fort like a heavy green fog. Bolt's leg that had belonged to a ballet dancer went up on pointe for a second. Then Bolt fainted. Luckily, he landed on Maxwell.

Holding his nose, Karl screwed the lid back on, as Patsy and Maxwell helped Bolt up.

"Good thing Dennis isn't here," Maxwell said. "He would have eaten everything in those jars by now."

"Where is Dennis anyway?" Patsy asked.

"I didn't invite him," Karl said.

Surprised, J.D. said, "Not cool. Why?"

"That's why I asked you to come over," Karl said. "I think Mr. Benedict is up to something." He took a breath. "And . . . I think Dennis might somehow be involved."

"No way!" Patsy said, shaking her head. "You're howling up the wrong tree."

Karl held up a paw. "It's not so crazy," he said. "Dennis is the one who found Mr. Benedict and brought him to practice. Suddenly, Coach Wyatt and Coach Virgil are fighting way worse than ever and not even showing up to practice or games."

J.D. was nodding his head. "And we're wearing the world's worst uniforms and eating the planet's most disgusting food."

"We have a sponsor so we can play in the game," Karl said. "But we can't win the game because of the sponsor."

"I can't believe Dennis would do anything to hurt the Scream Team on purpose," Patsy said. "But you might have a point about Mr. Benedict. I went online and I can't find F.I.B. anywhere."

"There's a way to find out if he's up to something," Karl said. "Mr. Benedict said he eats every night at the Road Kill Café. We can follow him from there."

The others agreed to the plan.

"Hold on! We should go in disguise." Maxwell grabbed a sheet and put it over his head. "Look! I'm a ghost! Boo, boo, boo."

"Dude," J.D. said, shaking his head. "I repeat, not cool."

Patsy rearranged her body parts, and even tried putting her foot on Karl's shoulder. But in the end they forgot about using disguises.

"We'll just stay out of sight and hope he doesn't spot us," Karl said.

By the time the five monsters got to the restaurant on Mange Street, Mr. Benedict was just leaving.

He glanced at his watch. "Oh! I'm going to be late!" they heard him say as he hurried along the sidewalk. Hustling to keep up, they followed Mr. Benedict into the haunted woods. The cloudy night made it hard to see.

Maxwell's wrapping got tangled on a branch and stretched out across the path like a clothesline. Patsy walked right into it and was split in two.

"Shhh!" Maxwell said really loudly.

"Who's there?" Mr. Benedict asked. He raised his snout and sniffed.

Karl and his friends ducked behind some bushes, right in the middle of a tongue-tickler nest.

"Who's there?" Mr. Benedict repeated. He plucked his whiskers nervously. *Ping! Ping! Ping!*

Wolfsbane! Karl thought. He didn't want to scare Mr. Benedict. He was just about to speak when—

Something moved in the shadows and a voice emerged. "It's just us," a kid said.

It was a Vampire! The whole Vampire team stepped into the moonlight, wearing their basketball uniforms.

Mr. Benedict seemed to have been expecting them, but he didn't relax. If anything he looked even more nervous. "Allan . . . why do we have to meet way out here?"

The head Vampire laughed. "We can't let anyone see that you're working for us, can we? Those weirdos on the Scream Team are already losers, you're just helping them realize it. In fact, you're really doing them a favor!"

That's it! Karl thought, and he shared a look with J.D.

The Vampires were behind the nutty ideas of Mr. Benedict. They were out to make the Scream Team lose!

A tongue-tickler was trying to pry its way into Patsy's mouth. She swatted at it and accidentally smacked Karl. He opened his mouth to say "Ow!" A tongue-tickler squirmed through his lips—

—he snapped his mouth shut. Too late.

"Hee-hee," Karl giggled.

"What's that?" Allan the Vampire asked. He looked right where Karl and the others were crouching.

"Uh-oh," Patsy said.

"Run!" Karl yelled.

The Vampires swept toward them in a wave of flapping wings. Karl and his friends raced back toward Mange Street. But the Vampires would probably catch them before they made it that far.

"Quick!" Karl said, and led the Scream Team to a nearby bog. They dove in and swam under a giant floating mushroom cap. There was only enough air down there for them to breathe for a short time.

After a few minutes, Patsy tied one of her ears to the end of some slimy pond grass and let it float to the top. "I don't hear anything," she said. "I think the Vampires are gone."

They swam back to the bank, where J.D. twisted the bog water out of himself like a wet cloth. "They didn't see us," he said, "but I think they're around. We have to get out of here before they come back."

"See you tomorrow!" Karl said as the other four monsters headed home. But Karl wasn't going home yet. He had another vampire to visit first.

CHAPTER 7
Grave Matters

Just after leaving his friends, Karl made his way through the dark shadows of the cemetery. Among the sounds of TVs and video games coming from six feet below, a vampire's voice floated up from a nearby grave. "Do I smell wolf? I think the delivery ghoul is here with dinner!"

Karl trotted quickly ahead. Dennis and his family lived in a big tomb cut into the side of the hill. Karl lifted a paw to knock on the steel grate when he heard Dennis yelling behind him.

"Fly, Squishy, fly!" the vampire said. Karl turned, but couldn't see him. He was hidden by a row of giant tombstones. Karl padded over and spotted his friend.

Dennis was standing behind a tombstone that was twice as tall as he was. Squishy, Dennis's pet rotten tomato, jiggled on its viney legs at his feet. Dennis scooped him up. "Ready, Squishy?" Squishy happily squirted red juice in reply.

"Okay," Dennis said. "Then . . . fly, Squishy, fly!"

Karl could see Dennis was practicing the Monster Shot. He had nailed a rotting basket to a dead tree that was a basketball court's length away. But why was Dennis practicing way out here? That was something to ask another time. Karl had bigger mysteries to solve . . . like how much Dennis knew about Mr. Benedict and the Vampires.

"Dennis, we've got to talk," Karl said, surprising Dennis. The vampire's eyes went wide. *Flip!* His wings popped out and he lifted off the ground.

"Hold on." Karl grabbed his legs to pull

him down. It wasn't easy. Dennis was getting stronger and better at flying. Squishy swung on a vine from Dennis's hand and fired streams of juice everywhere.

"Dennis!" Karl shouted. "It's me! It's Karl!"

Dennis stopped flapping and fell to the ground on his back. He sat up and Karl plopped down next to him while Squishy curled up in Dennis's lap.

"Sorry, Karl," Dennis said. "You scared me. What's going on? Why are you here?"

Karl took a breath, not sure how to say what he was thinking. "Are you trying to make the Scream Team lose?"

"What?" Dennis said, looking away and turning as red as Squishy. "That's nuts."

"Then why do you look so guilty right now?" Karl asked. When Dennis didn't answer, Karl plugged ahead. "The championship game is tomorrow. Our team is a mess. Is that what you're trying to do? Make us lose?"

Dennis seemed shocked. "No, of course not!"

"Why were you talking to the Vampires in secret?" Karl asked.

Dennis looked down again. "I can't say."

"*Can't* or *won't?*"

"I'm not supposed to, but I'm not sure why," Dennis said. "The Vampires told me I should bring Mr. Benedict to meet the Scream Team. That I should make sure he'd be our sponsor."

"Why would you listen to the Vampires?" Karl said. "They told Mr. Benedict to make sure that we lose."

"I didn't know that!" Dennis protested. "I thought we'd all win. The Scream Team would get a sponsor. And, if I do what the Vampires say, I'll get to play on their team." Then Dennis's voice became a little sadder. "They told me they'll pass the ball to me. And that I won't be sitting on the bench the whole time. They're my friends."

Karl couldn't believe his ears. "Dennis, the Scream Team monsters are your friends."

"I know," Dennis said. "But I might have to play

with monsters like me if I'm ever going to learn anything."

Karl didn't agree, but what could he say? Dennis had to do what made him happy.

Karl gave Squishy a pat, and said, "Okay, Dennis. But that still leaves Mr. Benedict. We're going to have to figure out what to do about him."

CHAPTER 8
Fangs for Nothing

The next night, Putridge Stadium was buzzing.

The Vampire fans had bought up most of the tickets for the big championship game. There were only a handful left for the Scream Team's family and friends. When Karl and his teammates came out to the court, he could hear his dad say "Way to go . . ." but only thanks to his wolf ears.

"Are we on our own?" Beck asked. There was no sign of Mr. Benedict or the Conundrums—and it was five minutes until game time. If the coaches didn't show up, they would have to forfeit the game.

"A forfeit might be for the best," Mike said as he tripped over his cape for the thirtieth time that night. Mr. Benedict had thrown away their old uniforms, and there hadn't been time to get new ones. They were stuck with these.

Dennis sat on the end of the bench, close to the Vampires. Karl was about to ask him what he'd decided, when Mr. Benedict came up the ramp onto the court.

J.D. started yelling "Boo!" and Patsy got so angry her head popped off.

"We know everything!" Maxwell yelled, not knowing he was talking to the water cooler instead of Mr. Benedict.

"Wait!" Mr. Benedict said. It was the first time he hadn't said something like it was a question. "You don't know everything. For one thing, I'm sorry I tricked you."

He sounded so sincere that Karl and the others went quiet. Then Patsy asked, "Why did you do it?"

Shrugging, Mr. Benedict said, "All my life I've wanted to be part of a team. But I was always too different. The Vampires said I could be part of their group if I ruined your team." He sighed. "But now that I know you, I want to help you."

Karl shared a look with J.D. and then asked, "Why should we believe you, Mr. Benedict?"

A little smile touched the mole man's face. "Because I have two monsters to back me up, and—"

"Surprise!" Virgil Conundrum shouted as he and his brother, Wyatt, popped up from behind the bench. Dennis shrieked and took off flying.

"Too soon, Virgil!" Coach Wyatt snapped. "You always say *surprise* too early!"

"I told the Conundrums the truth," Mr. Benedict said. "Wyatt was right all along. I *was* a spy."

"From now on, people better start listening to me!" Wyatt said.

"Don't look now," Virgil said with a wink, "but I think you have another mole on your face!"

"Where? Get it off! Get it off!" Wyatt yelled.

The coaches spun away from them with Wyatt slapping his own face and Virgil laughing.

"Looks like our coaches are back to normal," J.D. said.

"But *we're* not," Karl said, pointing down at the bells, whistles, and tap shoes. "Did you really throw away our old uniforms?"

Mr. Benedict nodded sadly. "And what's worse is that I don't have any money. F.I.B. was an L.I.E. Everything I spent came from the Vampires. If I had money, I'd sponsor the Scream Team, but . . ."

He didn't have to finish. After tonight's game the Scream Team wouldn't have a real sponsor and they'd be kicked out of the league. And not just for basketball—for all the sports they played. Just then the buzzer sounded.

The Scream Team's last game was about to start.

CHAPTER 9
Fly Blind

"Welcome to the JCML Championship Basketball Game!" Hairy Hairwell's voice blasted from the announcer's booth. "This slam-a-lama fest at Putridge Stadium is jam-packed with thousands of Vampire fans—and for the Scream Team? Not so much. The winner of tonight's contest will walk away with the Monster Trophy and b-ball bragging rights for the next year!"

A spotlight flashed onto the giant Monster Trophy up in the president's skybox. Karl started drooling. Made of rusty nails and chipped glass, it was the most beautiful thing he'd ever seen. Dr. Neuron was seated next to it. He waved to the crowd like a king.

"Frank the Cyclops was mysteriously poked in the eye by a tentacle and will not be reffing tonight's game," Hairy announced. "In his place, the honorable Dr. Neuron has appointed George the human fly as referee!"

Another spotlight popped up on George, who buzzed out to the middle of the court. Once there, George winked up at Dr. Neuron. The winking was hard to miss—George had a hundred eyes.

"Uh-oh," Karl said. "I think we might be in trouble."

"Get out there, Scream Team!" Wyatt snapped. "If we're going down, I say we go down big!"

With a new sinking feeling in his stomach, Karl clicked out in his tap shoes to play point guard. Patsy was the power forward. J.D., at small forward, and Maxwell, at shooting guard, joined them on

the court.

Bolt, at the center position, still seemed a little worried about the ball. He wouldn't listen when Coach Wyatt told him that basketballs couldn't feel. Finally, Virgil gave up trying to convince him and said, "Fine, but bouncing is what the ball was born to do. You're just helping it reach its goal in life!"

Now Bolt seemed ready when George tossed up the jump ball. The ref's flapping wings made a little breeze that blew the ball right into the hands of Allan the Vampire.

Then Allan flew down the court and scored inside. Edward the Vampire scored down low. And Ethel hit a three-pointer for the Vampires. *Bam. Bam. Bam.*

Just seconds into the game, the Vampires were crushing the Scream Team. Trying to break the Scream Team's cold streak, J.D. was going up for a three-pointer when Allan called out, "What's the net weight of gas from a Beaneater Hyena?"

Bolt's teacher's-pet arm shot up and blocked

J.D.'s shot. Allan grabbed the ball.

"Bolt sorry!" Bolt said to his teammates.

"It's okay, Bolt," Karl said, wondering, *How did the Vampires know that one of Bolt's arms came from a teacher's pet?*

Karl quickly learned that the Vampires knew *everything* about the Scream Team.

He called different secret Scream Team defensive plays, like Jellyfish, Stinkgrub on a Stick, and even Oozy Doozy. But thanks to Mr. Benedict, the Vampires knew all their plays.

And just as Karl went to grab a rebound, he saw that Mr. Benedict was sneaking off the court.

He must be too ashamed to stick around for a second longer, Karl thought. And Karl almost wanted to join him.

The Scream Team hadn't scored yet and the Vampires already had 18 points.

All the while, Dennis flitted nervously between the two teams' benches. He looked like he had to go to the bathroom, and Karl couldn't tell if he had made up his mind about which team he would root for.

Allan the Vampire scored and drew a foul, even though there wasn't a Scream Team player within twenty feet. When he missed the free throw, another Vampire snagged the rebound and put it back up into the net.

"Kaboom!" Hairy shouted. "The Scream Team is really struggling. Not much basketball going on for them."

The Scream Team couldn't get a possession that lasted more than two seconds. After Maxwell got the ball tangled up in his wrappings, Ethel stole it and bombed a three-pointer.

"Enough!" Coach Wyatt yelled, calling a time-out. But George the ref ignored him. Karl made a T with his paws. The ref ignored that, too, and the trouncing continued.

Samantha the Vampire faked a shot, then she drove baseline and dished to a cutter for the easy lay-up.

Finally, Patsy pulled off her legs and made a T with them. The ref couldn't act like he didn't see it this time, and blew the whistle for a time-out.

"There's no way we can win," Wyatt said when the Scream Team gathered around.

"Great pep talk, Coach," Mike said.

"They know all of our plays!" Virgil said. "Everything—forward and backward."

"That's it!" Karl said. "Maybe Mr. Benedict taught us something we can really use—"

The ref blew the whistle for the game to resume before Karl could explain. When they were back on the court, Karl waved his paw in the air and called, "Enoz eerht-owt!"

Bolt looked more confused than ever and Patsy switched her ears to make sure they weren't on the wrong side of her head. The first one on the team to understand was J.D.

He grinned at Karl and said, "Lap, gnikniht

doog!" which was *Good thinking, pal,* backward. He'd figured out that Karl was calling the two-three zone play in reverse like Mr. Benedict had taught them. Soon the rest of the Scream Team got it, too.

But it didn't click for the Vampires. They thought Karl was talking gibberish. They couldn't tell which plays he called until it was too late. And it made them furious.

Allan got in Karl's face and yanked the ball out of his paws. George blew the whistle, calling a foul against Karl. The monsters in the stands cheered.

Allan hit one free throw and missed the second. Karl snagged the rebound—

And raced down the court as fast as any werewolf on tap shoes ever has. *Tap! Tap! Tap!* He zigzagged around Samantha, nearly wiped out on the slippery soles, and went in sideways for a lay-up.

"Count it!" J.D. cried and drifted over to Karl so they could exchange high fives.

"Kablam!" Hairy shouted. "The Scream Team is on the board! But not everyone is happy about it!"

Allan rocketed down the court toward Karl and J.D. He flashed into a bat to really build up speed and then back into a kid. He hit Karl at full force—*WHAM!*—knocking him off the ground and out of his shoes!

CHAPTER 10
Time for T.R.U.T.H.

Karl spun through the air and smacked into the hard surface of the court ten feet below. For a second, he thought there was something wrong with *his* ears. He expected to hear the sound of laughter from the crowd.

But instead there were a few gasps.

"Ouch, that must have hurt," a beetle creature in the bleachers mumbled.

"Not cool," a flying dinobot muttered.

There were a few other murmurs in the crowd

and shouts from the Scream Team bench. Even Hairy seemed a little taken aback. "Huh, that was rough," he said over the speakers. And then, just like that, the crowd started cheering for the Vampires again.

Karl got up and dusted himself off, eyeing his tap basketball shoes. He was about to put them back on when he realized Allan might have done him a favor.

"Time to lose the shoes!" he told his team.

"No shoes?" Maxwell asked. "What will that do to my look?"

But Patsy was already kicking off her tap shoes and wriggling her scabby toes happily. "Oh yes!" And the rest of the Scream Team took them off, too.

Meanwhile, the ref had called a foul on Karl for "blocking" Allan, and the Vampire went to the line to take two. The Scream Team inbounded the ball and took it down the court. Patsy made a hook shot just as Alice the Vampire elbowed her in the nose. The ref didn't call it.

"Looks like the ref needs to keep at least one eye on the court," Hairy announced. "That foul was as clear as the nose now on the back of that zombie girl's head."

Moving much quicker without their shoes, the Scream Team started making headway. Karl kept calling the plays backward. J.D. drilled a baseline jumper for two more points. Maxwell used his wrappings as a slingshot, firing the ball at the backboard and scoring a much-needed three-pointer.

After Bolt blocked one of Alice's shots, the

Scream Team felt like they had a chance to get back in the game—

The Vampires were up 72 to 55 when they called time-out with eight minutes to play in the fourth quarter. As the Scream Team gathered around the Conundrums, an out-of-breath mole man gently pushed into their circle.

"Mr. Benedict?" Karl said, wiping the sweat out of his eyes. "What are you doing back here?"

Mr. Benedict smiled and held out his bag.

"Oh no," Beck moaned, grabbing his stomach. "More sandwiches?"

"No, look more closely," Mr. Benedict said. "It took some digging but I got them out of the dumpster."

Karl squinted. He could see the coffin lining poking out of the pack. "You have our old uniforms!"

Maxwell unspun some wrapping and they draped their capes over it, creating a little changing room. The uniforms were crusted with snail slime and pickled brains. But they happily put them on.

"I want to tell you something I should've when I was your coach," Mr. Benedict said quietly to the team. "Remember that what makes you different is what makes you stronger. And that's no F.I.B. That's the T.R.U.T.H."

The Scream Team took to the court looking like the team they should have been all along.

"It seems we've finally got our act together," Maxwell said as he passed the ball to Karl.

"But it's too late," J.D. said and pointed at the scoreboard and the ticking clock.

Karl shook his head and smiled. "It's never too late."

CHAPTER 11
And Then There Was Dennis

The Scream Team continued to break the Vampire zone. Karl and J.D. ran a pick and roll three times without a single basket from the Vampires.

"Stop them!" the Vampire coach shrieked at Allan and the other Vampires with 4:25 left in the game. "Time for Operation: Take Out Starting Team!"

"Uh-oh." Patsy gave Karl a worried look. "Please tell me that means something better than it sounds."

It turned out to be exactly what the Vampire

coach said. Desperate to win at any cost, the Vampires went from a monster-to-monster defense to mob-to-monster. It was like a five-on-one zone where all of their players on the court went after just one player on the Scream Team.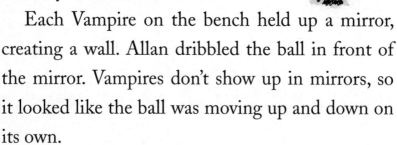

They started with Bolt.

Each Vampire on the bench held up a mirror, creating a wall. Allan dribbled the ball in front of the mirror. Vampires don't show up in mirrors, so it looked like the ball was moving up and down on its own.

Allan pretended to be the ball and said things like, "Oh please, oh please! My face ... ouch! Ouch! Ouch!"

Bolt freaked. "No hurt ball!" he shouted. He grabbed the basketball and ran to the locker room, refusing to come out.

"One down," Allan told his teammates, "four to go!"

Once the ref had found a new game ball, the Conundrums sent Beck in for Bolt at center.

Play started again, and the Vampires turned their focus on Patsy. They acted like they each had the ball. She tried to go in different directions and her arms, legs, and head flew off. The janitor had to come up with the broom to sweep her to the Scream Team bench. It would take her time to screw herself back together, so Mike went in for Patsy.

During all of this, the Scream Team still managed to score. With all five Vampires going after one player, the other monsters on the Scream Team were free to make baskets. Mike scored five points and Karl scored six more. In fact, they were catching up . . . they had 69 to the Vampires' 81. But the Vampires didn't seem to care. If their plan worked, there wouldn't be anyone left on the Scream Team to play.

As the Vampires flocked toward Maxwell near the Scream Team net, Karl snarled, "Leave my friends alone!"

"Don't worry," Allan said with a wicked grin. "We'll get to you soon, werewolf."

Always a flopper, Allan acted like he tripped. He fell fang-first onto the court. One of his sharp teeth pegged a strip of Maxwell's wrapping to the floor— and the mummy didn't see it.

"Don't move, Maxwell!" Karl shouted. That was a mistake. Maxwell hated being told what to do.

"What? Why?" he demanded, and started rushing around. His wrapping was still snagged on Allan's fang and Maxwell spun like a crazy top as it unwound. When he finally stopped turning, the mummy was buried in loose wrapping.

"My look is ruined!" Maxwell cried, and hurried to the team's bench, pushing the heaps of cloth in front of him. He'd need days to rewrap things just the way he liked them. Now just J.D. and Karl were left from the starting lineup. Coaches Conundrum put in Eric.

Out on the court, Mike fired off a gorgeous bounce pass to J.D., who drove to the net. He scored two points, which made the Vampires even angrier.

After the ref called another fake foul on Karl,

Allan went to the free-throw line.

"Hey, ghost, watch this," Allan said to J.D., waving the ball back and forth before he shot.

"Watch what?" J.D. said, his eyes following the ball.

"Wolfsbane!" Karl shouted. "J.D., watch out! He's hypnotizing you!"

Too late. J.D.'s eyes had glazed over. Grinning, Allan told him, "You are a sheet on a clothesline."

J.D.'s body turned square and flat and dangled off the ground.

"There's a storm!" Allan said. "A hurricane!"

As J.D. flapped all over the court, Allan took his two shots and made them both. The crowd loved it. The ref was laughing so hard, tears squirted out of all one hundred of his eyes.

"Stop it, Allan!" Karl growled.

"Okay, okay," Allan said, putting his hands up in the air. The vampire turned to J.D. "You're not a bed sheet anymore . . ."

Karl sighed in relief, then Allan finished his

sentence, ". . . you're a sheet of paper!"

When J.D.'s body went paper-thin and drifted, Allan continued, "And you're jammed in a printer!" J.D. jerked side to side for a minute, and then shot across the court, sliding under the bleachers. He was out of the game.

"Aw, does the ghost have a *boo-boo*?" Allan asked the spectators. "Now that's what I call a real basketball *jam*!"

As the crowd's roars of laughter crashed over him, Karl's eyes ran along the Scream Team bench. They needed one more player on the court or they'd have to forfeit. J.D., Patsy, and Maxwell were slowly putting themselves back together. And Bolt was still hiding in the locker room.

There was only one Scream Team monster left on the bench.

CHAPTER 12
Monster Shot

The whole Scream Team groaned.

"Looks like you're going in for J.D., Dennis," Coach Virgil said. For once, he sounded worried. Coach Wyatt just shook his head, his face red and sweaty.

The Vampires shared a couple high fives, thinking they'd won the game. And Karl knew why.

Either Dennis would play for the Scream Team—in which case he'd be so bad, he'd lose the game for them—or Dennis would side with the Vampires and lose the game on purpose.

One way or another, Dennis would win for the Vampires.

As the Vampire fans snickered, Dennis took a step onto the court. "Ish . . . ush . . ." he mumbled. He looked confused, like he couldn't believe he was actually in the game.

"All the reserves are in for the Scream Team," Hairy announced, not helping Karl's nerves. "If one more of their players gets knocked out of the game . . . it's all over for them."

Karl went a little ball-crazy. Beck waved his arms and Eric was constantly open. But Karl wouldn't pass the ball once he had it. He wanted to keep it away from Dennis.

Meanwhile, the Vampires continued their "Take Out Starting Team" plan. They focused on Karl and made squeaky sounds from all over the court.

"Stay tough, Karl," Patsy called from the sidelines as she screwed her head back on.

"Pass the ball!" Coach Wyatt shouted. "You can't win the game solo!"

With all the squeaking, Karl had a tough time hearing anything. Still, he wouldn't be distracted by the Vampires' tricks. Not tonight. Instead, he responded with a three-pointer.

"Yes!" Karl yelled, and pumped a paw in the air.

The Vampire coach called a time-out with thirty seconds left in the game.

"Way to go, Karl," Coach Virgil cheered when the team circled around him. "The score is 72 to 83. There's still time for you to win the championship."

"I don't know," Wyatt scoffed. "Not unless you monsters learn to trust one another out there, and actually share the ball."

As the coaches talked, Karl had a tough time concentrating. Now squeaking sounds were coming from *inside* the Scream Team circle. Had a Vampire snuck in?

No, it was Dennis! He was nervously squeaking his fingers against his fangs. Like Karl chasing his tail, this was something Dennis did when he was stressed-out.

Suddenly, it hit Karl how much Dennis just wanted to play basketball.

Trust one another.

The time-out was over. Back on the court, Mike bounced the ball off Eric to Karl. "Go, Karl!" Beck shouted. "Take the ball. We only have twenty-five seconds!"

Karl didn't hesitate.

It was time to trust his friend. And for the first time, Karl passed the ball to Dennis.

Dennis almost flubbed the ball as his wings popped out on his back. He swayed at the middle of the court, as if deciding which team to play for.

"Why did you do that, Karl?" Dennis asked.

Karl didn't say anything. No one did. The whole place seemed to be holding its breath.

Time was ticking down.

Dennis wiped the drool off his chin. His face went from fear to certainty. He cocked an eyebrow at Karl and dashed toward the Vampires' net.

"No, Dennis!" J.D. shouted.

Hairy Hairwell was nearly hysterical. "Dennis is going to betray the Scream Team! He is going to score against his own team!"

I don't think so, Karl thought, smiling.

Dennis didn't stop to shoot into the Vampires' basket. Instead, he dribbled into the space between the out of bounds line and the back of the backboard.

He planted his feet firmly on the ground. He was going for a Monster Shot.

"Stop!" the entire Scream Team shouted at the same time. Everyone except Karl.

"Go for it, Dennis!" Karl said, thinking of the game against the Ghosts, when Dennis had cheered him on.

Dennis looked at the ball and Karl knew he was imagining his rotten tomato pet. "Fly, Squishy, fly!" Dennis shouted.

The crowd laughed. And Dennis shot over the backboard and down the court. The ball sailed through the air and seemed to hang over the net for a second.

And then, *wift!*

No rim. Right through the net. A Monster Six-Pointer.

Ka-klam! The stadium roof nearly blew off from so many monsters shouting at the same time.

"Dennis has done it!" cried Hairy Hairwell. "He has nailed the impossible shot!"

Karl's heart leapt as the crowd continued to cheer, roar, and shriek. Looking dazed, Dennis was still under the Vampires' net.

"How'd you learn to do that?" Allan sneered at Dennis.

Dennis thought for a second, and then said,

"Hanging out with monsters who trusted in me."

When the game continued, the Vampires' fouls got even worse. They pushed and shoved Karl and his teammates, finally scoring one more basket.

Before Karl knew it, the clock was running out. The crowd started counting down, "Five, four, three, two, one!"

Karl drove to the hoop with a one-handed dunk. He made the shot just as the horn sounded.

"What?" Dennis said, looking around like maybe he'd ripped his pants. "What is it?"

The ball was still bouncing on the court, and then stopped. Up on the mega-screen, the score flashed: VAMPIRES: 85, SCREAM TEAM: 80.

"We lost," Karl said, barely able to believe the words himself. "The season is over and we lost the game."

CHAPTER 13
Game Change

Karl and his team stood stunned as the Vampires dumped a bucket of boiling slime over their coach's head.

They went through the post-game line with the Vampires, as the head of the JCML hustled down from the stands. Karl had never seen Dr. Neuron move so fast—or look so happy.

Waving to the crowd, Dr. Neuron just about skipped out to the middle of the court where a microphone and podium had been set up. He held a tentacle over his mouth, but he couldn't hide the grin on his face.

"Monsters, it is my great pleasure . . . and I mean happy, happy, oh-so-happy pleasure to present this trophy to the winners of this year's Junior Club Monster League Basketball Championship"—his tentacles pointed at the winning team—"the Vampires!"

The crowd went quiet, except for the crickets chirping. Karl always thought cricket monsters were a little annoying.

Allan strode out to take the trophy for his team. "Thank you," the Vampire said, bowing like he was a movie star getting an award. "Thank you!"

Now the crickets stopped chirping. Silence fell over the stadium. The monsters in the stands just stared at Allan.

"Uh . . ." Allan blushed and backed away from the podium.

Dr. Neuron didn't seem to notice, and continued, "In second place, we have this"—he pointed at Karl

and his friends—"this group."

"We're not just a group," Karl said. He trotted over to the microphone. "We're the Scream Team—"

Dr. Neuron pulled the microphone away. "Maybe you were once. But not anymore. Here."

He shoved a crumpled paper into Karl's paw. It was a used napkin from the Foul Feast diner, and someone had written *2nd* on it. Karl was stunned. He stood there staring down at the napkin. *This is what we have to show for all our hard work?*

"The Scream Team is no longer a team!" Dr. Neuron shouted, then pointed at Mr. Benedict. "This mole man is penniless and not a real sponsor. Therefore this group is no longer welcome in the JCML. They have played their last game!"

He stopped as if waiting for the crowd to go nuts. Still there was no sound.

"I know," Dr. Neuron said, nodding. "I too can barely speak due to the joy I feel. According to the rules, this ragtag mess of different monsters is finished. Let that be a lesson to all of you.

Winning is about being the same!" He turned back to the Scream Team. "Please leave the court forever. Now."

The crowd wasn't just staring anymore. They were glaring. The silence felt like a boulder rocking on the edge of a cliff. Karl could tell something was about to happen. And the Conundrums seemed to think it wouldn't be good.

"Come on, gang," Coach Virgil said. "Time to go."

The coaches hustled everyone toward the locker room. Karl hesitated. *This can't be it*, he thought. *No more Scream Team?*

Dennis came back and tugged on his arm. "We did our best, Karl. We can't stay—"

Plink! A monster in the crowd had tossed something and it hit Dennis in the face. "Ouch!" Dennis cried.

"Now they're throwing things at us?" Patsy said. "Let's get out of here."

"Hold on," Beck said. He slid a foot under the thrown object, flipped it up, and caught it. "It's a coin!"

Karl took the coin and held it up. Why would someone throw money at them?

Slap! One fin slapped another. *Thud!* The slap was joined by paws coming together. And then claws. Hands. Tails. Soon the whole crowd was clapping.

Plink! Plink! Plink!

Coins rained down on the Scream Team.

"What are you doing?!" Dr. Neuron waved his tentacles at the crowd. "Cease this nonsense immediately!"

A raw hot dog slapped into his face. Then a deep-fried pus bag. The crowd was flinging food at Dr. Neuron—and it was piling up around the Vampires, too. They turned into bats and flew out of the stadium, leaving Dr. Neuron alone on the court.

"They're throwing old treats at you, Dr. Neuron," Wyatt said, and Virgil added, "You could say it's a good time to . . ."

"Retreat!" Dr. Neuron shouted and scurried off the court.

Now the crowd really went crazy. Waves of cheers and applause washed over the Scream Team.

Mr. Benedict scooted around, gathering up the money. But there was too much for him to pick up. Maxwell and the other monsters used some of his unraveled wrapping to scoop up the change.

"You know what this means?" Karl said. "They love us!"

"Uh," Patsy said. "*Love* might be a little strong!"

There were still monsters making the thumbs-down sign, and a few threw oozing muck balls instead of coins.

"Okay," J.D. said with a smile. "The crowd might not *totally* love us, but they don't like the way the Vampires played the game."

"With this money," Coach Virgil said, "Mr. Benedict can be our sponsor. The Scream Team is back!"

"And Dennis is the one who really made the crowd see how great we are," Karl said. "He did something only my hero, Wolfenstein, could do!"

They all turned to look at Dennis. For the first time in weeks, Dennis smiled and said, "I did do it, didn't I?"

As an answer, Karl let out a howl for his friend. Then he and the others hefted the chubby vampire into the air. Dennis's flapping wings made him easier to lift. Still, even with Mr. Benedict helping, Dennis was hard to hold up. And soon they all collapsed into a giant pile of laughing, squirming monsters.

Karl had never been happier, surrounded by his friends. But something was missing. He poked his head out from the mound and spotted the Conundrums a few feet away. "Come on, Coaches!" he called.

"No way." Coach Wyatt shook his head. "There could be spies in that pileup!" Then, before Virgil could say a word, Wyatt snarled, "Oh, why not!"

And the Conundrums jumped into the heap with the rest of the Scream Team.

Scream Team

DENNIS THE VAMPIRE

Number: 11 Looks like my fangs upside down!

Position: Benchwarmer Hey! Not cool!

Best Move: Toward the dessert table

   No! It's my Monster Six-Pointer

Favorite Food: See above Anything but steaks!

Hobby: Training his rotten tomato Squishy is the

Basketball Hero: Karl the Werewolf BEST pet

   #0 on the court but my #1 friend

Favorite saying: Sho so fit!

   Is that how I sound saying "Go for it"?

Place to Improve: Flying Still winging it with my wings!

Talent: Turning into a bat It's not just when I'm scared

Nickname: Bat boy How about Mr. Big Shot?

STILL HUNGRY?

Sink your teeth into the first Scream Team!

Scream Team

The Werewolf at Home Plate